HEL/CH

SCOULAR ANDERSON lives and works in Scotland. He studied Graphic Design at the Glasgow School of Art and worked as an illustrator for London University. He has also worked as an art teacher and has been a writer and illustrator of children's books for over 16 years. *Space Pirates and the Treasure of Salmagundy* is Scoular's first book for Frances Lincoln.

For the staff and pupils of Strone Primary School, Argyll, who road-tested these maps.

Space Pirates and the Treasure of Salmagundy
copyright © Frances Lincoln Limited 2004
Text and illustrations
copyright © Scoular Anderson 2004

The right of Scoular Anderson to be identified as
the author and illustrator of this work has been
asserted by him in accordance with the Copyright,
Designs and Patents Act, 1988.

First published in Great Britain in 2004 by
Frances Lincoln Children's Books, 4 Torriano Mews,
Torriano Avenue, London NW5 2RZ
www.franceslincoln.com

First paperback edition 2006

British Library Cataloguing in Publication Data
available on request

ISBN 10: 1-84507-380-0
ISBN 13: 978-1-84507-380-0

Printed in Singapore

9 8 7 6 5 4 3 2 1

Find out more about the adventures of the
Space Pirates on Scoular Anderson's website:
www.scoularanderson.co.uk

Space Pirates
and the Treasure of Salmagundy

Scoular Anderson

F

FRANCES LINCOLN
CHILDREN'S BOOKS

Space pirate ship, **Sleepy Sheep**, is zooming through a galaxy...

On board is Pirate Captain Tosca...

Navigator Needlespune...

Engineer Dogzboddi...

the cabin boy, Coleslaw...

and the computer, IDA (short for Intergalactic Direction Assistant).

I think this is the planet we're supposed to come to. It's time to check the treasure map disk, Coleslaw!

Aye, aye, Captain!

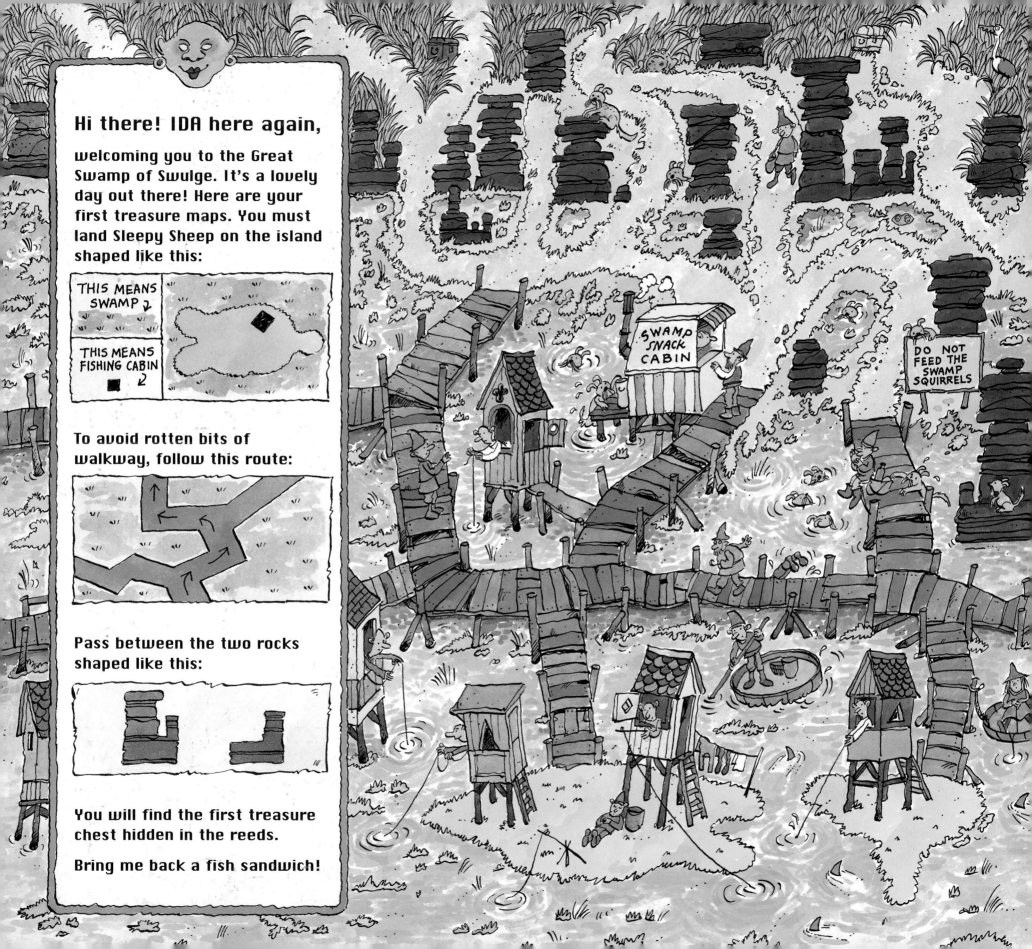

Hi there! IDA here again,

welcoming you to the Great Swamp of Swulge. It's a lovely day out there! Here are your first treasure maps. You must land Sleepy Sheep on the island shaped like this:

THIS MEANS SWAMP ↙

THIS MEANS FISHING CABIN ↙

To avoid rotten bits of walkway, follow this route:

Pass between the two rocks shaped like this:

You will find the first treasure chest hidden in the reeds.

Bring me back a fish sandwich!

SWAMP SNACK CABIN

DO NOT FEED THE SWAMP SQUIRRELS

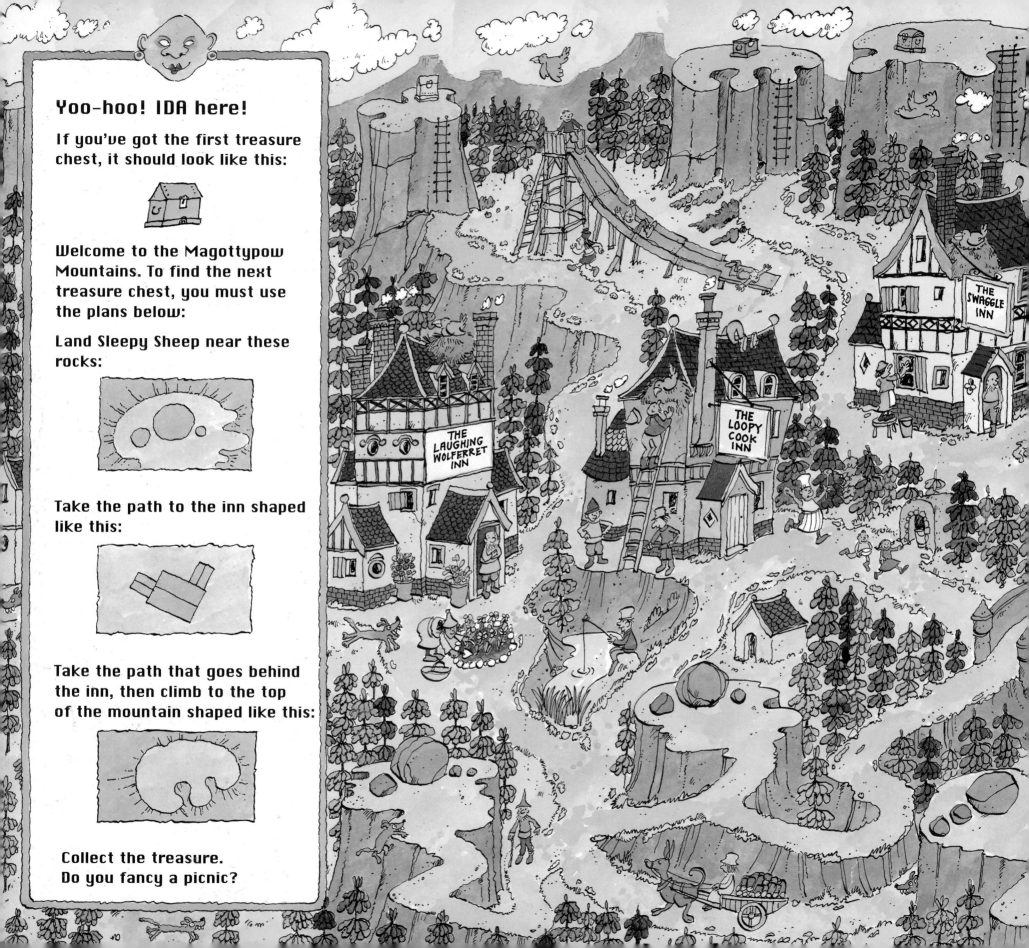

Yoo-hoo! IDA here!

If you've got the first treasure chest, it should look like this:

Welcome to the Magottypow Mountains. To find the next treasure chest, you must use the plans below:

Land Sleepy Sheep near these rocks:

Take the path to the inn shaped like this:

Take the path that goes behind the inn, then climb to the top of the mountain shaped like this:

Collect the treasure.
Do you fancy a picnic?

Hi-ya! IDA speaking.

If you got the right treasure chest from the mountain, it should look like this:

You are now at the Wittery Waterfalls. Here's what you have to do:

Land Sleepy Sheep on the back of this fall hog (it's OK, they sleep for months).

Climb to the top of the right-hand steps. Take the left-hand path as far as the plumberry-picker's hut.

Cross the bridge that goes behind the waterfall.

Go to the cave that's second on the left.

Find the treasure. Anyone for a plumberry sandwich?

Halloo! IDA here!

If you got to the right treasure chest at the waterfalls, it should look like this:

You are now arriving at the Diskko Desert. Land Sleepy Sheep on this flat rock.

Use the compass to find the right directions.

NORTH
WEST
EAST
SOUTH

Go north to the fallen porridge palm tree.

Go east to the pointy rocks.

Go south to the oozy pond.

Go west to the porridge-seller's tent. In there, you will find the next treasure chest.

The porridge is delicious, especially with a sprinkling of sand.

PORRIDGE PALM INSPECTORS' OFFICE

DIGGZI'S DE LUXE PORRIDGE

PANDDA'S PERFECT PORRIDGE

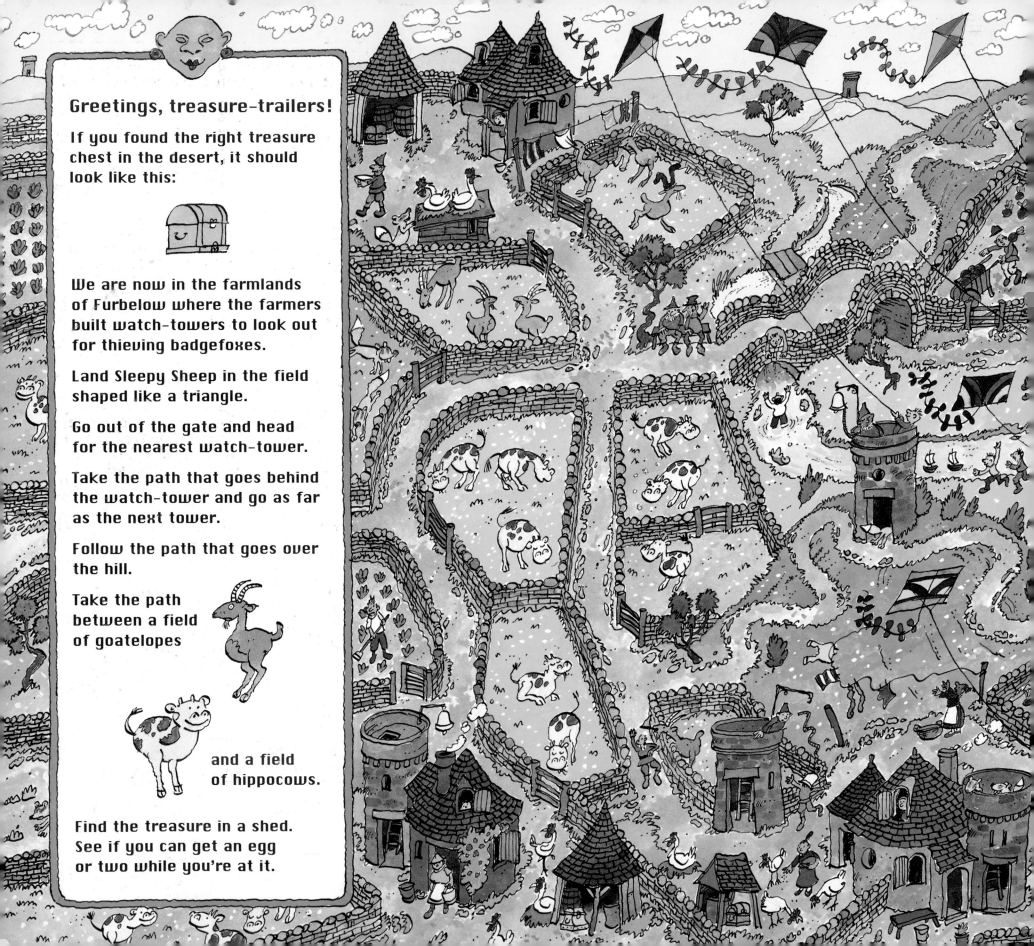

Greetings, treasure-trailers!

If you found the right treasure chest in the desert, it should look like this:

We are now in the farmlands of Furbelow where the farmers built watch-towers to look out for thieving badgefoxes.

Land Sleepy Sheep in the field shaped like a triangle.

Go out of the gate and head for the nearest watch-tower.

Take the path that goes behind the watch-tower and go as far as the next tower.

Follow the path that goes over the hill.

Take the path between a field of goatelopes

and a field of hippocows.

Find the treasure in a shed. See if you can get an egg or two while you're at it.

Howdie, pirate pals!

If you found the right treasure chest in the farmlands of Furbelow, it should look like this:

Below is a map of the Layzee Lagoons. Use it to help you find the next treasure chest.

THIS MEANS LIGHTHOUSE	THIS MEANS MUD	THIS MEANS SAND	THIS MEANS PEBBLES
●	▬	▬	▬

Land Sleepy Sheep beside the lighthouse marked X on the map.

Walk to the end of a sandy beach.

Take a boat across to the round island.

Hop across the stepping stones then walk to the end of another sandy beach. Pick up the treasure in the lighthouse.

Bring me back two jellyfish pies, please.

BOAT HIRE

BOAT HIRE

JELLYFISH SCOOPS FOR HIRE

BEST JELLYFISH PIES Sold Here!

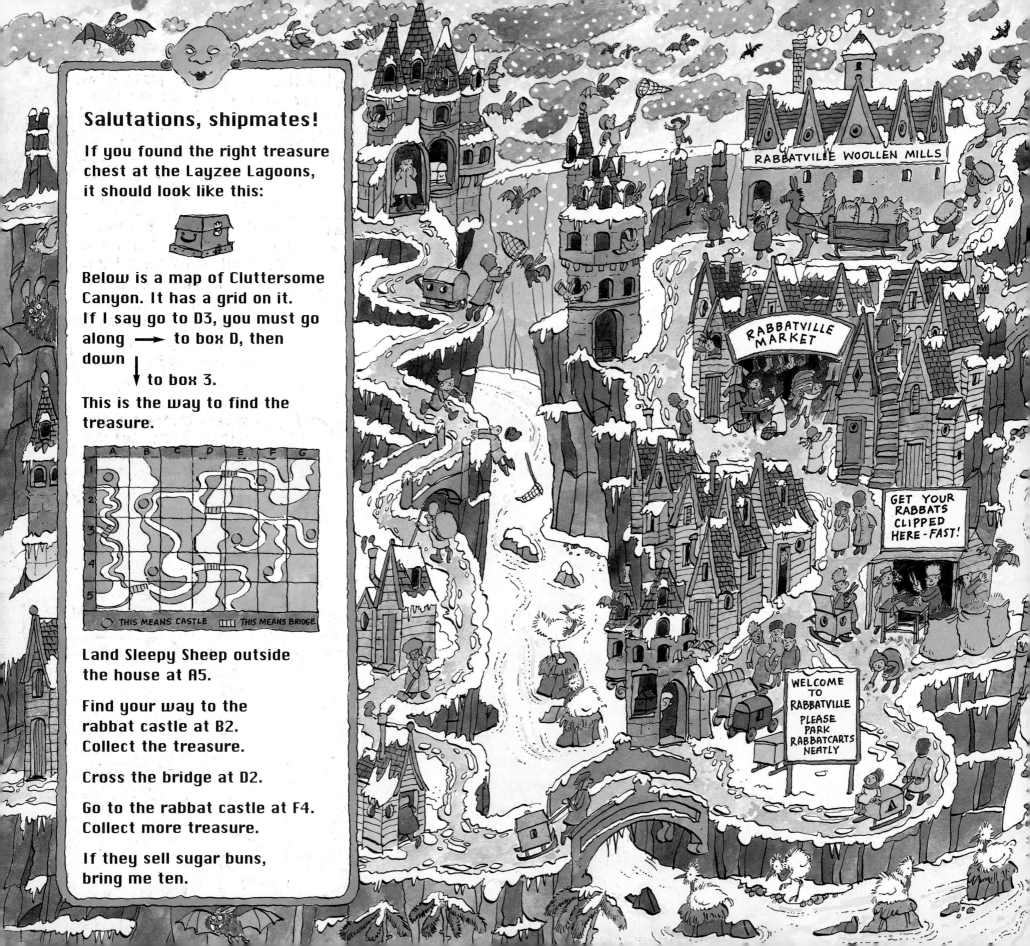

Salutations, shipmates!

If you found the right treasure chest at the Layzee Lagoons, it should look like this:

Below is a map of Cluttersome Canyon. It has a grid on it. If I say go to D3, you must go along ⟶ to box D, then down ↓ to box 3. This is the way to find the treasure.

THIS MEANS CASTLE ▭ THIS MEANS BRIDGE

Land Sleepy Sheep outside the house at A5.

Find your way to the rabbat castle at B2. Collect the treasure.

Cross the bridge at D2.

Go to the rabbat castle at F4. Collect more treasure.

If they sell sugar buns, bring me ten.

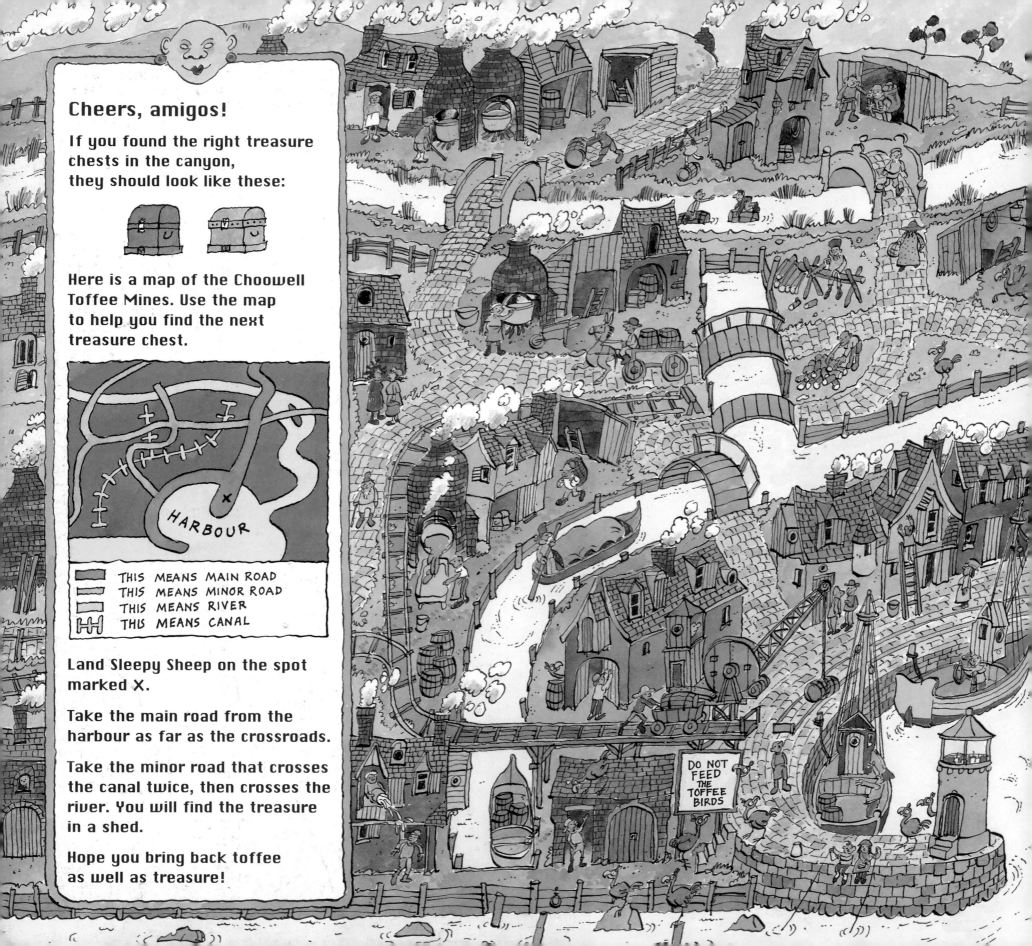

Cheers, amigos!

If you found the right treasure chests in the canyon, they should look like these:

Here is a map of the Choowell Toffee Mines. Use the map to help you find the next treasure chest.

THIS ▬ MEANS MAIN ROAD
THIS ═ MEANS MINOR ROAD
THIS ▭ MEANS RIVER
THIS ⊞ MEANS CANAL

Land Sleepy Sheep on the spot marked X.

Take the main road from the harbour as far as the crossroads.

Take the minor road that crosses the canal twice, then crosses the river. You will find the treasure in a shed.

Hope you bring back toffee as well as treasure!

HARBOUR

DO NOT FEED THE TOFFEE BIRDS

Howdie-doodie, shipmates!

If you found the right treasure chest at the mines, it should look like this:

We are now near a swaggle pitch. The Swaggle Cup final is taking place. You will need something to measure with if you want to find the next treasure chest. Here is a scale.

0 1 2 3 4 5
HOGSTEPS

Land Sleepy Sheep behind the round goalpost.

From the goalpost pole, take 10 hogsteps towards bunker number 2.

Take 6 hogsteps towards the square goalpost.

Take 15 hogsteps towards the referee in the blue box.

Take 12 hogsteps towards the red referee's box. You will find the treasure in the bunker to your right.

Do you think there will be sandwiches after the match?

HABDASH AMAZERS	v	MUDDYFLATTS DAZZLERS
FLIPS	5	POINTS	2
TROUNCES	11		0
RUN THROUGHS	2		5
TOTAL	18		7

REFEREE

REFEREE

Gizmo, you guys!

If you found the right treasure chest on the Swaggle pitch, it should look like this:

It's time to take a look around Muddpye Market. Use the town plan to help you find the treasure.

Land Sleepy Sheep under a tree beside the fountain marked X.

Go in the direction of the arrows and pick up the first treasure chest in the shop at the top of some steps.

Continue to follow the arrows and pick up treasure at the fountain marked XX.

Follow the arrows until you reach the stables marked XXX and pick up the treasure chest.

That completes the treasure hunt. Hurry up! I'm starving.

MORE BOOKS IN PAPERBACK AVAILABLE FROM FRANCES LINCOLN CHILDREN'S BOOKS

Dotty Inventions and Some Real Ones Too
Roger McGough
Illustrated by Holly Swain

Have you ever wondered who invented velcro, Frisbee
or the parachute? It was Professor Dotty Dabble of course
and she wants to win first prize in the competition for best
invention. But her robot sidekick Digby is not so sure all these
amazing ideas belong to Dotty and he sets out to
discover whose inventions they REALLY are!

ISBN 978-1-84507-117-2

Until I Met Dudley
Roger McGough
Illustrated by Chris Riddell

Have you ever wondered how a toaster works or how
a fridge keeps cool? Dudley the techno-wizard dog travels
from the furthest realms of fantasy to the fascinating
world of technology to discover the workings
of familiar machines.

ISBN 978-0-7112-1129-2

Fly on the Wall: Roman Fort
Mick Manning and Brita Granström

Patrol with a windswept centurion, eavesdrop in the smelly
toilets and visit a tasty Roman banquet! This fly-on-the-wall
sketchbook is packed full of information about Roman life
from the latest archaeological discoveries.

ISBN 978-1-84507-124-0

Frances Lincoln titles are available from all good bookshops.
You can also buy books and find out more about your favourite titles,
authors and illustrators on our website: www.franceslincoln.com